Pastels and Jingle Bells

Heavenly Bites Novella #1

◆

Christine S. Feldman

Printed by CreateSpace

Pastels and Jingle Bells first published via Kindle Direct © 2013 by Christine S. Feldman

ISBN-13: 978-1544941622

ISBN-10: 1544941625

Cover Design by - Elaina Lee

Cover Images - © Fotolia

For anyone who appreciates a little humor mixed in with their holiday season—

CHRISTINE S. FELDMAN

CONTENTS

ACKNOWLEDGMENTS

Thank you to the friends, family, and readers who have been so supportive—I love you guys!

❖ Chapter One ❖

IT WAS PROBABLY INVITING the worst kind of karma to be contemplating murder during the holiday season of all times, but that didn't faze Trish Ackerly in the slightest as she stared through her bakery's storefront window in shock.

It was *him*. Ian Rafferty, bane of her junior high school existence. She'd know that face anywhere, despite the changes in it. Sure, he was a couple of feet taller now and certainly broader shouldered, but as he glanced away from the winter scene she had painted on the window only yesterday and at a passing car that whizzed by *much* too fast on the busy city street, the profile he presented to her confirmed it. Yes, it *was* him. That same nose, the odd little scar above his eye, the familiar way he quirked his lips…

Her eyes narrowed. Ian Rafferty. That miserable, mean-spirited little—

Then he turned his face back to the window, and Trish gasped and dropped to the floor before he could spot her staring at him.

"What on earth are you doing?" came Nadia's voice from behind the counter.

Trish huddled behind a tall metal trash can and glanced up through her dark bangs at her startled friend and business partner only to remember belatedly that they had company in the shop, namely wizened little Mrs. Beasley, whose startled eyes blinked at her from behind enormous tortoise-shell spectacles.

Well, there was little help for it now. "That guy," Trish hissed, jerking one thumb in the direction of the window. "I know him!"

Both Nadia and Mrs. Beasley peered intently through the glass. "Mmm," said Nadia appreciatively a moment later. "Lucky you, girlfriend."

"No, not lucky me! That guy made my life a living hell in junior high. He's a jerk, he's a bully—"

"He's coming in here, dear," Mrs. Beasley interrupted her, with obvious interest in her voice.

With a squeak of alarm, Trish shuffled hastily behind the counter on her hands and knees and hunched into as small and inconspicuous a ball as she could.

Nadia blinked. "Trish, are you out of your—"

"Sh!"

"Oh, you did *not* just shush me—"

"SHH!" Trish insisted again, knowing full well that she'd pay for it later, and then she pulled her head down into her shoulders as much as her anatomy would allow.

The bell on the door jangled cheerfully then, and a gust of cold air heralded Ian Rafferty's arrival.

"Hi, there," Nadia greeted him brightly, surreptitiously giving Trish's foot a little dig with one of her own. "Welcome to Heavenly Bites. What can I get for you?"

"Cup of coffee would be great for starters," came a voice that was deep but soft, and far less reptilian than Trish expected. She cocked her head slightly to better catch his words and heard the unmistakable sound of him blowing on his hands and rubbing them together to warm them. "Cream, no sugar."

"Sure thing, honey."

"Your window art," his voice continued, and Trish straightened ever so slightly at the mention of her work. "It's fantastic. Can I ask who painted it?"

"Absolutely," Nadia returned, turning her attention to getting the coffee he requested. "My business partner, Trish."

"Is she around, by any chance?"

Nadia glanced down at where Trish sat scrunched up and did what Trish thought was a very poor job of suppressing a smirk. "She's, um, indisposed at the moment. Why do you ask?"

"I've got a couple of windows that could use a little holiday cheer. Think she might be interested in the job?"

Nadia gave Trish another brief sideways glance.

Trish shook her head frantically.

"Tell you what. Leave me your number, and we'll find out." Nadia stepped out of reach before Trish could smack her leg.

"Great, thanks. Here's my card."

"I'll see that she gets it, Mr.—" Nadia glanced at the card. "—Rafferty. Here's your coffee, and you, sir, have a very nice day."

The bell on the door jingled again, and Trish cautiously poked her head up long enough to verify that Ian was indeed gone. She then ignored the fascinated look Mrs. Beasley was giving her and fixed an icy stare on Nadia. "I'm going to kill you. How could you do that?"

Nadia tossed her dark braids over her shoulder. "Hmph. Shush me in my own shop…"

"I don't want to talk to that guy! I don't want to have anything to do with him."

4

"He seemed nice enough to me," her friend returned, shrugging unapologetically. "And easy on the eyes, too."

"And single," put in Mrs. Beasley eagerly, one wrinkled hand fluttering over her heart. "No wedding ring."

"Of course there's no ring! No woman wants to marry the devil!" Trish sank back down onto the floor and leaned back heavily against the shelves behind her.

"He *used* to be the devil," Nadia corrected her, examining the business card he had handed to her. "Now he's 'Ian Rafferty, Landscape Architect'. And he's a paying customer, Trish. Face it, you could use the money."

"Forget it. I'm not so hard up that I'd go crawling to Ian Rafferty for a job." Trish scowled and folded her arms across her chest. "I have my dignity, you know."

"Yeah? Why don't you get up off the floor and tell me all about your dignity."

"Oh, shut up," Trish muttered, getting to her feet and snatching the card from Nadia's hand. Wadding it up, she tossed it in the direction of the trashcan and stalked into the bakery's kitchen.

◆ ◆ ◆

HER AIM MUST HAVE been off, because the crunched up card was lying on the floor by the trashcan when she locked up that evening. It caught her eye as she was reaching for her coat, and her gaze darkened. A hundred different memories swirled up inside her head...

Ian shoving her twelve-year-old self down for no reason at all as he walked by her at recess; Ian yanking on her braid, laughing at her snaggletooth; Ian teasing her in the hallway and calling her names—Patty-cake, wasn't that what he used to call her? A baby name that made her cheeks burn with embarrassment every time she heard it. She'd learned to hate the name Patricia and switched to going by Trish once she moved out on her own.

She'd gotten her teeth fixed, too. Put on a couple of pounds in most of the right places, cut her hair and darkened it a few shades. Learned to take care of herself. All in all, Trish had come a long way. She hardly bore any resemblance at all to the goofy kid Ian had tormented years ago, she thought as she stooped to pick up the business card and prepared to drop it in the trash. How aggravating, then, that her brief glimpse of him today should leave her so hot under the collar, as if it had all happened yesterday instead of nearly twenty years ago. And then old instincts had kicked in and sent her scurrying for cover! Wonderful. She'd be thrilled if today's unexpected encounter was the last she ever saw of him.

But then again...

Her hand froze in place over the trashcan.

...maybe she was being presented with a once-in-a-lifetime opportunity here.

Trish slowly straightened and stared at the card between her fingers. Back in junior high, Ian had disappeared before she'd summoned up enough courage to tell him exactly what he could do with himself. He'd moved away overnight, leaving her relieved but also a quivering mass of insecurities.

What if...

Trish smoothed the wrinkles out of the card enough to read the name and phone number on it. A little thrill ran through her as a scene played out in her mind.

What if she actually confronted the jerk and told him off, just like she used to fantasize about doing as a kid? And even—if she was honest about it—a few times as an adult, too. And now she wasn't some poor little goofy preadolescent, despite the way she had behaved this afternoon at the sight of him. She could show him just exactly the confident, attractive, and poised woman she had become. Ha!

When a little voice in the back of her head tried to suggest that confident, poised women didn't need to go around proving that they were confident and poised, she chose to ignore it. She wasn't *insecure*. Absolutely not. She was merely seeking appropriate closure to a painful period in her life. And if that closure happened to involve a certain triumphant comeuppance, well, what was so wrong with that? Opportunities like this didn't come along every day. It was a gift. To turn her back on it would be downright crazy. Ungrateful, even.

Pulling out her cell phone, she dialed the phone number on the card before she could lose her nerve.

Ian answered on the third ring, and his voice momentarily startled her with its deepness. "Ian Rafferty."

Trish took a deep breath and forced a breeziness into her voice. "Mr. Rafferty? My name is… Trish. I believe you're looking for me."

❖ Chapter Two ❖

"IT'S A SILLY IDEA, girlfriend."

"It's not silly," Trish corrected Nadia from across their favorite booth in La Bella Rosa. "It's inspired." She pointed her fork at her friend. "I think you're just all sour grapes about it because you've never had a chance to confront some jerk from *your* past like this."

"I don't need to. I always confront them in the present. You should try it sometime."

Trish ignored her and took a bite of her linguini.

Nadia sighed and shook her head. "Sounds like a waste of a perfectly good hunk of man flesh to me. Come on, Trish. You guys were kids. Kids do stupid things. Just let it go."

"Not stupid. Cruel. This guy tormented me all the time back then. It's like he singled me out or something. I was the butt of all his jokes—" She ticked the examples of evidence off her fingers one at a time. "He pulled my hair, tripped me in the halls, called me names—"

"Who called my darling girl names?" an indignant voice demanded hotly, and both Trish and Nadia glanced up to see "Pop" De Luca, proud owner of La Bella Rosa and patron grandfather to half the neighborhood, standing beside their booth. He wiped his meaty hands on the apron tied around his substantial middle and glowered, which would have been more effective if his wispy white hair didn't frame a face like a cherub's.

"Hey, Pop," both women greeted him at once.

"Don't 'hey Pop' me. If somebody's not treating one of my two favorite girls right, I want to know about it. Give me his name, I'll talk to the *pazzo* and set him straight."

"His name is Ian Rafferty, but I'm going to set him straight myself, Pop. Thanks anyway." Trish patted the old man's hand.

He seemed unconvinced because his scowl remained in place. "This bum isn't somebody you're dating, is it, *cara*? If he is, he's got to go." Pop jerked a thumb in the direction of the door.

"He did go," Nadia put in wryly. "Eighteen years ago."

The old man's scowl faltered as his brow furrowed in confusion.

"But now he's back," Trish said firmly. "And I intend to give him the verbal thrashing I should have back then."

"And when are you putting this master plan of yours into action?" her friend asked.

"Saturday." Trish took another bite. Pop's pasta was the best in the city, which was probably why she and Nadia ate here so often—which was itself probably the reason why Pop had practically adopted them both. Maybe it was the pasta talking, but she was feeling bolder by the minute. "I'm supposed to drop by his house to talk about his job offer, but I've got a very different speech in mind."

Pop's eyes lit up. "His house, huh? So you know where this bozo lives?"

"Forget it, Pop. I'm not telling you where it is."

"But—"

"Nope. Don't worry." Trish smiled a confident smile. "I've got it covered."

And she pointedly ignored Nadia's eyeroll, choosing to look out the window at the lightly falling snow instead.

◆ ◆ ◆

MUTTERING UNDER HER BREATH, Trish tugged the hem of her short little black skirt down as far as it would go and shivered. The tights she wore offered little warmth or protection from the brisk December wind, but she told herself that hypothermia was a small price to pay for the satisfaction she was about to achieve.

Eat your heart out, Ian Rafferty, she thought, and then stumbled when the heel of her pump caught in a crack on the sidewalk. Yanking it free, she nearly slipped on a patch of ice and did a wild sort of sideways shuffle with her arms windmilling until she recovered her balance.

Feeling her cheeks bloom with heat, she threw an anxious glance toward the house that sat at the address Ian had given her. She saw no sign of him, so hopefully he had missed her impromptu little Ice Capades rendition. Abandoning any attempt at a sashay, she settled for tiny mincing steps and proceeded cautiously toward the entrance of his home.

It was smaller than she expected. Somehow the bold lettering on the card made her picture someone who wore double breasted suits and power ties and was rolling in money, but the house up ahead was a rather small single-story brick home that looked like it had been built at least fifty years ago.

But the yard, small as it was, put all the other yards on the street to shame. Considering Ian's line of work, Trish supposed she shouldn't be surprised. Because it was his, she wanted to dislike it, but the way each part of the yard flowed seamlessly into another while still retaining its own special charm—

on the verge of winter, no less—she had to begrudgingly admire it.

Unless, of course, she turned her attention away from the enchanting yard and onto something else, like the speech she had rehearsed several times during the night as she lay awake, too wired with adrenaline to sleep.

Well, well. Ian Rafferty. I'll bet you don't remember me, do you? Allow me to refresh your memory.

In her mind's eye, the words were followed by a swift kick to his shins, or maybe someplace a little higher. Not that she really planned to resort to violence, but a girl could dream. She reached for the railing beside his front steps and started up them, her mind still on her triumphant entrance.

Little Pattycake's all grown up now, and—

"Who are *you?*"

The sullen, small voice coming from somewhere below her made Trish gasp and jump. She wobbled precariously in the high heels that did wonders for her legs and derriere but precious little for her balance, and then her grip on the railing saved her at the last minute. "What the h—"

A little girl's wary brown eyes stared up at her from where she sat mostly hidden in the shrubs by the side of the house.

"—eck," Trish amended just in time. She willed her heart rate to slow back down to normal. "Yeesh.

Who am I? I'm the person who's cheated death twice today in these heels."

"What?"

"Nothing. I'm here to see Mr. Rafferty. He lives here, right?"

The girl just scowled at her and pulled the knitted hat she wore further down over her ears.

"Chatty, aren't you?" Trish commented, thinking that despite her limited experience with children, she was fairly sure it wasn't common to find one skulking around in shrubbery.

The child withdrew further into the bushes without another word, rustling branches and twigs as she went, and in a moment she was completely out of sight.

Trish blinked. "O-kay." Shaking her head, she turned her attention to the door in front of her and smoothed down a stray wrinkle or two in her skirt before raising her hand to knock.

Well, well. Ian Rafferty. I'll bet you don't remember—

The door opened before she could knock and suddenly Ian stood there, no more than three feet away from her. All of Trish's rehearsed words vanished from her mind.

"Hi," Ian greeted her. "I caught you through the window coming up the steps."

Remembering her slip on the pavement, Trish cringed inwardly.

"You must be Trish. Right on time." He held out his hand with a smile. "I'm Ian. Thanks for coming all the way over here. I hope it wasn't too much trouble?"

Reacting out of habit, Trish automatically stuck out her own hand for him to shake before she could think better of it. Her mind continued to draw a blank. Despite the familiarity in his features, Ian Rafferty up close had leaner lines in his face than he'd had as a boy. The scar above his eye was still visible but fainter, and yes, the nose was the same, but he had grown into it and lost any gangly quality he might have once had. The shortness of his current haircut suited him much more than the long brown mop that had once hidden most of his face like a surly curtain, and the overall effect was—she grudgingly admitted to herself—not bad.

But the devil could take many forms, after all.

Ian's fingers closed around hers, and Trish tried not to stiffen at the contact. She hastily withdrew her hand from his. "No, I—not at all." The words slipped from her mouth before she could stop them, a dogged testament to her parents' tireless efforts to bring up a polite young lady. Crud, she thought. This was not the speech she had practiced. She had to get things back on track before she lost her righteous momentum. "I—"

"Please come in," he invited her, stepping aside to let her enter. "You must be freezing. It's like the Arctic out there today."

For a moment she considered launching into her rant right then and there on his front porch, but that made it much too easy for him to simply slam the door shut in her face midway through it. She had not driven all the way down here to risk *that*.

Besides, the icy wind up her short skirt was freezing her nether regions off. No woman could deliver a proper tirade under these conditions. With a curt nod, she crossed the threshold, careful not to touch him as she brushed past.

Sudden warmth enveloped her as she stepped into a small living room that was tidy but bland in its lack of color. She couldn't quite suppress a grimace. No bright accents to cheer the place up, no framed photos—nothing on the walls except for a single still life painting of a bowl of fruit. Really? she thought as she eyed it critically.

The only other attempt at decoration that she could see was a sparsely-trimmed miniature Christmas tree on an end table. The room's one saving grace was the crackling fire in the fireplace that looked old enough to be part of the home's original construction, but it wasn't enough to make the place truly inviting. The contrast with the charming yard out front was downright astonishing.

Ian's hand touched her shoulder, and Trish gasped and pulled away from him. She turned to see him blinking at her in surprise.

"I'm sorry," he said, sounding abashed. "I was just going to ask if I could take your coat."

"Oh." She felt her cheeks flush. "Um, no. I'll hang on to it."

"Okay." After an awkward pause, Ian tried again. "Can I get you something to drink? Coffee maybe?" He looked wary as he asked it, as if he wasn't sure if she might respond oddly to this, too.

Her flush deepened. "No, I'm fine." A moment later, since good manners dictated it, she added grudgingly, "Thanks."

This was not going at all as planned. The longer they spent on pleasantries, the harder it was going to be to say what she had come here to say. She was supposed to show him how poised and desirable she was now. So much for poised, she thought ruefully. Maybe she could still salvage the desirable part. As he turned to gesture at his front window, she unbuttoned her coat and slipped it off her shoulders.

"So this is one of the windows I was hoping you could do something with," he said. "Along with one of the back bedrooms—" As he turned back to her, he did a double take, and his voice stumbled over his words. "Uh, down…down the hall."

"I see." Trish felt the first small surge of triumph since arriving on his doorstep. Apparently the deep vneck of the clingy red sweater she had chosen to wear had achieved the desired effect. It showed off more cleavage than she normally liked to share with the rest of the world, but today she had made an exception. Pursing her lips, she went over to stand next to him and pretended to examine the dimensions of the windowpane.

After his initial startle, he didn't seem to know where to look but finally settled on staring very intensely at the glass.

The balance of power had finally shifted in her direction. Thank heavens for feminine wiles, she thought happily. It was time to make her move. Turning to face him directly—and leaving him little choice but to face her directly as well, although he seemed very careful not to let his gaze drop anywhere lower than her chin—she injected some steel into her voice. "Mr. Rafferty, I'm sure your windows would look great with a little paint on them."

"Ian."

"But I came here—what?"

"Call me Ian, please."

"I—fine. Ian. But the real reason I came over here today was to tell you something."

A shadow of dismay crossed his face, stronger than Trish would have expected over mere window art. "Something's come up? I understand the holidays are a busy time, but if you could find some way to fit me in, I'd pay you whatever you think is fair, Miss—

I'm sorry, I don't think I caught your last name on the phone last night."

Because she hadn't offered it. She'd preferred not to risk sparking any memories of the old Patricia Ackerly until the new one was standing right in front of him in all of her dolled up, push-up bra'd glory. She lifted her chin high and plunged ahead "My last name is Acker—"

The shrill ring of a cell phone cut her off mid-name, and Ian pulled the offending object out of his pocket.

Trish felt a flicker of annoyance. Seriously? Was he really going to take a call right when she was in the middle of talking to him? Well, of course he was. He was Ian Rafferty.

But he only frowned at whatever number he saw displayed on the phone before turning it off and sliding it back into his pocket.

Oh, she thought, somewhat mollified. But only somewhat.

"Sorry. You were saying?"

She took a step closer to the window and turned sideways to allow him a chance to better appreciate her profile before she let him know the full extent of her disdain. "I was saying that the reason I came here today was to tell you that you—" Trish stopped and frowned.

For Pete' sake, he wasn't even looking at her. His attention was drawn to something outside the window instead. Apparently her sweater wasn't cut low enough after all. Her eyes narrowed. She was never going to get this speech off the ground at this rate.

"Would you excuse me for a moment?" Without waiting for her answer, Ian hurried grimly out through the front door.

You've got to be kidding me, Trish thought incredulously as she stared at the empty space where he'd been standing a second ago.

And then she turned around and did a double take of her own as she glanced out the picture window.

The little girl from the shrubbery sat on the curb in front of the house, shoulders hunched as she scuffed the toe of her boot at some unseen thing on the street. Ian approached her slowly and sat down beside her. The little girl merely hunched her shoulders higher up around her ears and didn't appear to respond when he spoke to her. After a moment Ian sighed and gently rested one hand on her head before leaning over to kiss the top of her cap.

Trish's eyes widened.

Could it be...the girl was his? Ian Rafferty had spawned? Suddenly the child's sullen attitude seemed a lot more understandable.

Her eyes widened further.

Wait—then was he married? Was there actually a Mrs. Ian Rafferty in the picture?

Suddenly the shortness of Trish's skirt felt awkward if not entirely unsuitable for the occasion. This was not the way to meet anybody's missus, not unless one was potentially looking to start a catfight. Heat blossomed in her face again, and she hastily put her coat back on to cover her exposed cleavage.

As she clutched her coat closed, she watched Ian scoop the girl up in his arms and carry her toward the house. Despite her standoffish manner a moment ago, the child clung to him tightly and buried her face against his neck.

An unexpected pang hit Trish.

Ian entered the house with his daughter still cradled in his arms and headed toward the hallway. "Could you hang on a second?" he asked Trish softly. "I'll be right back."

Wordlessly, she nodded, and he disappeared down the hallway with the girl.

Trish blinked after them. Ian Rafferty was a father. And judging by what she'd just witnessed, maybe not such a bad one, either. This was her childhood nemesis? Somehow it didn't seem possible.

Ian returned a minute or two later, his expression troubled and his hands shoved deeply into his pockets. Something about the pose reminded her very much of the Ian from her childhood. He had never looked very happy then either. "My daughter,

Kelsey," he offered, looking at a loss for words. "She's having a hard time lately. Misses her mother, that sort of thing."

"Oh?" Trish mumbled brilliantly, wishing desperately that she had thrown Ian's business card into the trash after all.

"Yeah." He cleared his throat, and despite the carefully neutral look on his face, there was a slight edge to his voice. "She just got remarried. Doesn't call Kelsey much anymore."

"Oh," Trish repeated, softer this time.

"She's having a tough time at school, too. Other kids just don't seem to…" Ian trailed off and started again. "The thing is, Miss Acker, I was hoping the window art might be a way to draw her out and cheer her up a little bit."

"Look, Mr. Rafferty, I don't think—"

"She loves to paint, too. I'm kind of grasping at straws here, I know, but I just thought—Well, there's a quality in what you do that I haven't seen in a long time, something that just seems to leap out at you, and I was hoping you could help give my daughter a little holiday fantasy." Ian smiled a self-deprecating smile that didn't quite make it to his eyes and waved a hand at the underwhelming Christmas tree in the corner. "As you can probably tell, holiday cheer isn't my strong suit."

Her mouth opened and closed again as she struggled to process what he was saying.

This was all wrong. She was supposed to be marching out triumphantly from his house right about now while Ian watched in shock and dismay, humbled by the righteous fury she rained down on him. How on earth had things veered off in this direction?

His jaw clenched as if he wanted to say something more but had bitten his tongue to stop himself.

Her anger toward him seemed to have dissipated right about the time she saw him pick up his daughter so tenderly, but that didn't mean she had to get involved in the situation any further than she already was. His little girl's troubles were sad, yes, and maybe not completely unfamiliar, but it really was none of her business, she insisted desperately to herself as she felt her resolve weakening. She didn't owe Ian Rafferty anything.

He continued to wait for a response, his expression growing more and more discouraged. It was then she noticed the tiny dark spots on the collar of his shirt and realized that was where Kelsey had hidden her face when he carried her. Tiny wet spots, as if from tears.

Crud.

"Yeah," Trish sighed in resignation. "I'll paint your windows."

CHRISTINE S. FELDMAN

❖ Chapter Three ❖

"SO HE STILL HAS no idea who you really are?"

Trish restocked cupcakes on a tray and placed it back into the glass-fronted case where customers could see the treats and be tempted to indulge. She avoided Nadia's gaze. "Right."

"And you're going back there tomorrow to start on his windows?"

"Yes, I am."

Her friend started to laugh.

Trish shot her a dirty look. "I'm so glad you find all of this so funny. Pass me that platter of cream puffs, would you?"

"What happened to 'I'm going to make him drool, and then I'll squash him like a bug'?"

Arranging the cream puffs next to the cupcakes, Trish mumbled something.

"What was that?"

"I said I changed my mind. You were right, I was wrong. Satisfied? He's not the jerk he used to be."

"No?"

"No." Trish paused and stared thoughtfully at the store window she had painted, the one Ian had admired. Something about it leaped out at him, he'd said. A part of her was shyly pleased about that. Not many people seemed to notice the detail she put into it. Or if they did, very few bothered to say anything about it. "He's actually kind of... not awful."

Nadia grinned slyly. "Not awful?"

"Rein it in, woman. I'm not saying I like the guy. I'm just saying maybe he's not evil incarnate after all."

"I see. So he's just a single dad who's a devoted father, he's got his own business, and he looks as yummy as anything we sell here. That's all." Nadia leaned her elbows on the counter, her eyes twinkling at Trish. "Ooo, girlfriend, I have a good feeling about all of this."

"Hey, I just feel sorry for his kid, all right? I'm painting his windows, and then I'm getting out of Dodge. That's it."

"Uh huh. So what are you wearing to paint tomorrow? Mini skirt again, or thigh-highs and a divide-and-conquer bustier?"

Trish calmly made a rude gesture and went back into the kitchen to start on a batch of lemon scones while Nadia's laughter followed her.

◆ ◆ ◆

THE NEXT DAY TRISH chose a turtleneck that came up so high it practically covered the lower half of her face. Paint-splattered jeans, a bulky coat, and safely flat-bottomed boots finished off the ensemble. To top it off, she held a spiral notebook in front of her chest like a shield of modesty. If Ian noticed the complete one-eighty she'd made in her wardrobe choices when he opened his door to her knock, he gave no sign—although he did seem more relaxed about making eye contact this time. Too bad Trish wasn't.

"Hi," Ian greeted her. There were dark circles under his eyes as if he hadn't slept well, but he smiled nevertheless and rubbed a hand over his face, looking surprised to find morning stubble there.

Rough night? Trish couldn't quite bring herself to return his smile, but she nodded her head in response and even managed to maintain eye contact for a full two seconds before averting her eyes to look past him. "Hi."

He stepped back to let her enter. The fire was crackling pleasantly again, and the warmth it gave off was a welcome relief from the blustery cold outside.

This time Ian made no attempt to reach for Trish's coat, but she could have sworn she saw his mouth twitch as if fighting a smile when she removed the coat herself and draped it over the back of a chair. Remembering her behavior the other day, her face turned warm for a moment from more than just the fire.

Ian cleared his throat, and the twitch disappeared from his lips. "Coffee?"

Trish nodded again. If nothing else, at least drinking it would give her something to do besides struggle to make polite conversation. "Thanks."

"Kitchen's this way. Kelsey," he called out as he passed the hallway. "Miss Acker's here."

Acker. She had neglected to correct him the other day. She started to open her mouth to remedy the situation, then paused. Why bother? After a couple of days, they'd go back to being strangers again, and in the meantime there was something comforting about the anonymity the phony name gave her. Patricia Ackerly was a tongue-tied mess around Ian Rafferty, but Trish Acker could be anything she wanted. At least for the next few days.

She followed him warily into the kitchen and sat down at the table toward which he waved a hand in invitation.

"Cream and sugar?" he asked, reaching for a bubbling coffee pot.

Another nod. God help her, could she not get two words out? Something, *anything*—Her eyes searched the kitchen unsuccessfully for inspiration. She could do this. She was a confident, poised woman. "So…"

He held out her coffee to her. "Yes?"

"Cold out, huh?" *Oh, good grief.* Scintillating stuff. Maybe she could follow up with an insightful comment about how the coffee was hot and the table was hard.

She was saved from trying to come up with anything else by the arrival of Ian's daughter. The girl appeared in the doorway and eyed Trish as if sizing her up, and Trish found herself sitting a little straighter under her scrutiny. The child couldn't have been more than six or seven, and her jaded expression looked out of place on her young face. Scooping her long brown hair behind her ears, she plopped herself down in the chair opposite Trish and stared at her. "Where's your paint?" she demanded.

"Try again, Kelsey," Ian suggested wryly, taking a sip of his own coffee.

Kelsey sighed a long-suffering sigh and frowned. "G'morning," she said grudgingly.

"Hi," Trish returned, feeling woefully out of her element. "Paint's in the car."

"Why?"

"Because I can't start painting until you tell me what to paint."

"Oh," the child said, apparently satisfied.

Trish set her notebook down on the table and pulled a pencil from its spiral spine, prepared to sketch. "So a little Christmas fantasy, huh? You like reindeer? Snowmen?"

"I hate snowmen."

"I beg your pardon?" Trish blinked, taken aback. Who on earth hated snowmen?

Off to the side, Ian sighed.

"Snowmen are stupid," Kelsey explained as if it was obvious.

"Oh. Okay. Well, what about reindeer?"

The girl made a face.

"Santa? Candy canes? Christmas trees?" Trish got an eyeroll in response. "I see. Why don't you tell me what you *do* like then."

Kelsey stared thoughtfully into space for a moment. "I like zombies," she said finally.

"Zombies?" Unable to help herself, Trish threw a startled glance in Ian's direction. What had she signed on for here?

But he seemed as blindsided as she was, because he nearly spit out his coffee. "Zombies?" he repeated, coughing and sputtering as he stared at his little girl. "What do you mean *zombies*?"

"They're cool," she insisted, folding her arms across her chest. "Everybody likes zombies."

"Not for Christmas, they don't."

Trish got a mental picture of zombies in Santa hats and cheery scarves caroling around a Christmas tree, and a hiccup of laughter escaped her before she could help it. Both father and daughter looked at her in surprise. "Sorry," she said hastily, forcing a serious expression onto her face. "So we're going for a Tim Burton kind of Christmas then?"

"No," said Ian.

"Yes!" said Kelsey at the same time, her eyes lighting up.

Her father gave her an incredulous look. "You don't even know who Tim Burton is."

"Somebody who likes zombies, right?"

"Let's forget the walking dead, Kels."

"But you said I could decide what we painted!"

Ian set his coffee cup down on the counter and rubbed his head as if it ached. "Yes, honey, but I figured the fact that it shouldn't be anything that gave the neighborhood kids nightmares was understood."

Trish didn't quite catch whatever it was Kelsey muttered under her breath, but she thought it sounded something like "serve 'em right."

Her eyes met Ian's over the head of his daughter, and her unexpected sympathy for him caught her off guard. He looked utterly bewildered and at a loss as to what to suggest next. There was something about the sight of a helpless male that brought out her nurturing instinct, so despite the fact that she didn't have any bright ideas either, Trish plunged ahead. "So your dad says you're an artist," she said to Kelsey, praying she would throw Trish a bone.

The girl glanced at her father, who nodded encouragingly at her, and then back at Trish. "I'm not an artist. I'm just a kid." But her voice lacked conviction.

"That's the way most artists start out. Can I see some of your stuff?"

Kelsey stared at her for a long moment, and then she finally said, "Okay" in a voice that was much softer than anything Trish had yet heard from her. Sliding off her chair, she slipped silently from the room.

Ian took a deep breath and then let it out slowly as if dazed. "My baby girl likes zombies? How did that happen?"

"Give it a few years."

"What?" he asked, startled as he turned his attention fully onto Trish. "Why?"

"Because then it'll be body piercings and tattoos, and zombies will seem like nothing in comparison."

He blanched at her words and looked suddenly ill. "That's not even funny."

This time it was Trish's mouth that quirked upward as it fought against the urge to smile and lost. She tried to hide it by taking a sip from her coffee cup.

But Ian spotted it anyway. "You have a sadistic streak in you, don't you, Miss Acker?"

"Little bit," she agreed, unrepentant.

He stared speculatively at her for a moment as if surprised at the flicker of humor in her—she was fairly surprised herself—and then grinned a slow, appreciative grin that sent a peculiar sort of tingle through Trish. Picking up his coffee cup again, he raised it in mock salute and took a drink.

His daughter reappeared in the doorway clutching an assortment of papers in all different sizes. She hovered there for a moment with a shy look on her face that instantly made Trish forgive her for her earlier attitude. "May I see?" she asked the girl, setting her coffee aside and giving Kelsey her full attention.

Kelsey shuffled forward and placed her collection of pictures on the table in front of Trish.

Trish leaned forward to examine them, lifting them up one at a time with the care and respect she remembered craving so much when she was not much older than Kelsey. They were done in crayon, pencil, marker, paint—one even looked like it was done with colored chalk—and they showcased some of the standard little girl fare like animals and flowers along with occasional firework bursts of random color. No zombies that Trish could tell, but there were a fair number of dragons and elves, judging by the pointed ears. "These are great. Lots better than anything I did at your age. You must practice a lot, huh?"

The girl looked at her as if trying to determine whether or not she was sincere. Something in Trish's manner must have satisfied her, because she finally relaxed and nodded.

"Look, maybe we could do some kind of compromise," Trish suggested. "You take zombies off the table, and I'll promise not to paint any snowmen or reindeer, okay? Maybe we could do a Christmas in Fairyland theme instead—" She retrieved her pencil and notebook and started sketching roughly. "—with a castle over here, and maybe a dragon and a couple of elves…"

Kelsey's face brightened with interest, and she moved closer to examine Trish's drawing. "And a wizard?"

"Sure, if it's okay with your dad."

"And a griffin? Could we have one of those?"

Trish blinked and tried unsuccessfully to summon up an image in her head. "A what?"

"A griffin," the girl repeated, her enthusiasm growing by the second. "I like those best."

"I… well, I'm afraid I don't really know much about those."

"That's okay," Kelsey assured her, taking the pencil from her and starting a sketch of her own. She frowned in grim concentration and bent over the paper. "I do. I'll teach you."

"Oh. Okay," Trish agreed, willing her amusement not to show on her face for fear Kelsey would interpret it as mockery. "Thank you."

Kelsey nodded but didn't look up.

Biting her lip to keep from smiling, Trish glanced up and met Ian's eyes. There was a softness in his gaze as he shifted it from his daughter to Trish, and out of view of Kelsey, he mouthed the words *thank you*.

Trish felt that odd sort of tingle again and turned her attention back to Kelsey's drawing. "Well, then," she said with mixed emotions swirling inside her, "I guess we have a deal."

CHRISTINE S. FELDMAN

❖ Chapter Four ❖

"I THINK WE MAY have gone overboard with the elves," Trish said a few hours later as she examined the results of her handiwork and Kelsey's on the front window. "Looks a little like a Tolkien fan convention."

"It's perfect." Kelsey eyed the fairyland scene before them with a look of almost smug delight on her face, her paintbrush carefully held aloft so as not to drip. "Wait until Dana sees it."

"Friend of yours?"

"*No,*" the girl returned so emphatically that Trish turned to look at her in surprise. "She's in my class." Kelsey gestured vaguely down the street. "Lives over there. I *hate* her."

"Hate?" Trish repeated. "Why?"

"She's mean. So are her friends."

Memories of junior high and a young Ian swirled to the surface of Trish's memory. "How are they mean?"

Kelsey looked away from the newly painted window and played idly with the paintbrush in her hands. "They just are," she said softly.

Feeling a pang of sympathy, Trish took the brush from the girl and set it out of the way with her own so she could begin putting away the paints. "They pick on you, huh?"

"They say stuff about me." The child's voice dropped further so that Trish barely heard her. "And about my mom."

Trish frowned, wondering now about Ian's reference to his ex-wife and her absence in her daughter's life. With a little imagination and a lot of spite, some kids could take something like that and run with it. "That stinks," she said finally, wishing she could think of something more profound to say. "Did you tell your dad about it?"

"My teacher called him."

"She did? That's good."

"No, it isn't. She called him because I punched Dana in the nose. Then I got in trouble."

"Oh." Although her first instinct was to high-five the girl, Trish managed to maintain a solemn expression. Encouraging vigilantism in the first grade was probably not the best idea. "Well, you've got more guts than I did when I was a kid, I'll give you that."

Kelsey just shrugged and pressed her lips together in a tight line.

Woman and child stood silently side-by-side, contemplating the window art as snowflakes began to fall around them.

"It will get better," Trish said finally. "The whole Dana thing."

"It will?"

Trish turned her head to look down at the girl and found her looking back up at her earnestly. "Yeah. I promise. Hang in there."

Kelsey turned her face back toward the window.

"In the meantime," Trish continued, moving closer to the window and studying it, "I'll bet we could sneak one zombie into this picture if we made it real small. Right here, behind this tree. What do you think?"

"Really?" Kelsey brightened. "Could we give it long blonde hair?"

"I take it Dana's a blonde, huh? Okay, blonde it is. Hand me that yellow, would you?"

Someone cleared his throat, and both Trish and Kelsey jumped and looked up to see Ian standing on the porch, watching them. "How's the painting going, ladies?"

"Fine," Trish and Kelsey both said at the same time, a little too quickly. They exchanged a furtive look.

"Mmm," he said noncommittally, and Trish thought his lips might have curved slightly. "Weather's taking a turn for the worse—and you two both look like Rudolph anyway. Why don't you call it quits for the day?"

The dismay on Kelsey's face struck Trish as rather touching. Maybe she was growing on the girl after all despite her earlier efforts to foist snowmen and reindeer on her. Seeing Kelsey open her mouth to protest, Trish hastened to speak first. "He's right, we probably should. I don't know about you, but I can't feel my toes anymore. I'll come back in a couple of days to do the other window, okay? And maybe a few last minute details on this one."

"Can't you come tomorrow?" Kelsey asked, her disappointment obvious.

"Got a shift to work at my bakery." Trish saw the gleam of sudden interest in Kelsey's eyes and made a mental note to pick out some pastries to bring with her next time.

"Go on inside and thaw out, honey," Ian told his daughter. "I'll help Miss Acker clean up."

"Can I watch cartoons?"

"One hour."

The arrangement must have met her approval because Kelsey nodded and hurried up the steps, pausing just long enough to wave goodbye to Trish—almost shyly—before disappearing inside the house.

Ian turned back to Trish.

"It was just going to be one zombie," she said. "Two, three inches tall, tops. No one would even know—"

"Miss Acker."

"—that it was—Yes?"

"You gave my daughter a wonderful day today. Thank you for that."

"Oh. You're welcome."

Ian took the steps slowly as he approached her, and as he closed the distance between them, Trish noticed he must have shaved off his earlier stubble at some point while she was working outside with his daughter. The thought ran through her mind that maybe he had gone to the trouble because Trish was there, and she was disconcerted to realize that the possibility intrigued her.

He stopped a couple of feet away from her and examined the wintry fairyland scene on the window. "Nice," he commented. "I like the troll lurking with the candy cane under the bridge."

"Thanks."

"Sort of a blend between ominous and festive."

"Totally what we we're going for."

Ian turned to look at her and grinned. "She likes you," he said after a moment, the humor in his smile fading as he studied her.

Trish was suddenly very curious about what he saw when he looked at her that way, or at least what he thought he saw. "I like her, too."

"And what you said to her, about Dana—" Ian stopped, distractedly running a hand through his hair and leaving it just tousled enough to look inviting.

Inviting? Where had that come from?

"I know she appreciated it," he finished finally. "I appreciated it, too."

"How long were you standing there?"

"Not long, but long enough."

The two of them stood there for a minute, not quite looking at each other, until Trish finally cleared her throat. "I should probably get these things put away."

"Right, let me help you with that."

They both reached for the same paint jar at once, drew back to let the other go first, and then repeated the whole routine again before Ian coughed behind his hand in what might have been a smothered laugh. "I'll start on the other side," he suggested, and Trish could only nod.

He carried her buckets of supplies to her car for her despite her assurances that she could manage just fine, and then walked her into the house so she could rinse her brushes out in the kitchen sink. They stood beside each other there, Trish rinsing each brush's bristles until the water ran clear over them, and Ian pressing them dry with a paper towel as she handed them over. Neither said a word, and the only sounds were from the running water in the kitchen and the television in the living room as Kelsey watched her cartoons.

"So… Tuesday then?" Ian asked her finally as they finished, and he handed the brushes back to her.

"Sure," said Trish, trying to ignore the way the brief contact of his fingers with hers made her skin feel warmer. "Back window's smaller, too, so it shouldn't take as long."

"Thank you again, Miss Acker. I mean it. It was wonderful to see her smiling today."

"Trish," she heard herself say. "You can call me Trish."

Ian started to open his mouth as if to say something more, then seemed to think better of it.

Good idea, Trish thought, and then she nodded a quick goodbye and left.

CHRISTINE S. FELDMAN

❖ Chapter Five ❖

"TRISH?"

"Yes?" Trish answered absently, staring out the bakery's front window at the busy city street but not really seeing it.

"Since when do apple-pumpkin turnovers have chocolate chips in them?"

"Huh?" Turning, Trish saw Nadia in the kitchen doorway holding a tray of said turnovers in her oven-mitted hands, a bewildered look on her face. She did a double take. "Did you say chocolate chips?"

"Well they sure aren't raisins, girlfriend. Too bad. Raisins would have tasted better."

Dismayed, Trish took one of the offending pastries and tore it in two to taste it. She made a face and threw the rest away uneaten. "How did I manage to do that?"

"That's the kind of thing that happens when you can't get a guy out of your head."

"You're nuts. I'm not thinking about Ian."

"I never said it was Ian." A slow grin spread across Nadia's face. "Interesting that you did, though."

Trish frowned and turned to pick up a towel and wipe down a counter that was already spotless.

"You're starting to like this guy."

"No. I'm just... confused."

"About what? Which end of him to start nibbling on first?"

Trish wadded up the towel and threw it at Nadia, who avoided it easily and continued grinning. "You're not helping."

"Sorry."

"No, you're not."

"You're right, I'm not." Nadia came over to lean against the counter beside Trish and give her a companionable nudge. "Okay, talk. What's eating you?"

"It's just that he used to be such a jerk, and now he's..." Trish trailed off, feeling her cheeks growing warmer. "Not. And I wasn't expecting it, that's all."

"But that's a good thing, isn't it? I mean, that he's turned out to be a nice guy after all?"

"Sure, but it was a lot simpler to just hate him from afar."

"And he's gone and ruined that. The creep."

"Well, he kind of has. How am I supposed to act around him now? He's being all nice and funny and likeable, and now I'm starting to be nice back to him, and what's that supposed to lead to?"

Nadia delicately raised a single eyebrow, something she did much better than anyone else Trish had ever met. "I can think of a few things, including one or two that involve whipped cream and finger painting. How is this a problem?"

"Well, for one thing, he thinks my name is Trish Acker."

"So tell him the truth. He'll probably laugh."

"And just sweep the past under the rug? Somehow that doesn't feel right. Like I'd be letting down victims of school yard bullies everywhere." Trish rubbed her head and sighed. "I don't know. Like I said, I'm confused. *And* I'm getting a headache now. See? Nothing but trouble already."

"Go take some aspirin and lie down." Nadia gave her a gentle shove in the direction of the kitchen and its back room. "And don't overthink things. Life's too short to let your past screw up your future."

"What is that, Zen wisdom?"

"L.L. Cool J, I think."

"Ah." And then Trish headed off to find the aspirin.

◆ ◆ ◆

IT WAS SILLY TO waste time analyzing the situation, Trish decided the next morning as she pulled a carefully wrapped plateful of cupcakes from out of her fridge—the ones she had made yesterday just for Kelsey and decorated with leftover Halloween accents like plastic spiders and vampire teeth. Analyzing things to death served no useful purpose since she planned to finish the window painting today and would therefore have no reason to see either Ian or Kelsey again. She could make a graceful exit and wish them well, and then that would be that. No more headaches, and no more confusion.

She sighed then, feeling a whole lot less relieved by that thought that she had expected.

Ridiculous, she told herself, hastily grabbing a paper she had printed out from her computer the night before, a very special paper, and thrusting it into her pocket as she put her coat on.

Her cell phone rang, startling her. It was a little early in the morning to be receiving calls from anyone she knew. She frowned in confusion at the phone number displayed on it before recognizing it as Ian's. "Hello?"

"Trish? There's a problem."

Twenty minutes later, Trish stood beside Ian outside his house and stared at the mess that someone had made of his front window. Parts of the scene she and Kelsey had painted the other day were still visible, but most of it was masked behind what appeared to be random splatters of paint and—"What is that, raw egg?"

"I don't know, maybe. Somebody had a field day with it, though."

Trish turned to look at him. His eyes flashed with anger as his gaze traveled over ugly splashes of bright orange and blue that ruined a castle Kelsey had spent over an hour painstakingly creating. "Was it that Dana girl?"

He shrugged, his jaw taut. "Her parents swear it wasn't. Who knows? Could have just been random. Sometimes punks just stumble onto something beautiful and decide to wreck it for no reason."

It wasn't the first time someone had tampered with a window she'd painted, but experience made it no less aggravating. And the disappointment she felt at the sight of the vandalism was not so much on her own behalf anyway as it was for the little girl who had worked so happily on it with her. "Is Kelsey okay?"

"She's crying in her room. Won't come out."

"Can I talk to her?"

He closed his eyes, and Trish sensed the helplessness he was feeling. "You can try."

Trish felt a fleeting impulse to lay a hand on his shoulder or give it a comforting squeeze, but she lost her nerve, so instead she turned to go inside.

She made her way down the hallway to a closed door that had to be Kelsey's, judging by the assortment of stickers and stencils decorating it. Knocking, Trish called out softly, "Kelsey? It's Trish. Can I come in?"

There was no answer, and even when she pressed her ear to the door, all she heard was the creak of a mattress as if someone on it had rolled over to face the other way or possibly hide her head under a pillow.

Now what? Trish wondered, keenly feeling her lack of experience with children. She put a hand on the doorknob to tentatively test it and was not surprised to find it locked. "Kelsey?" she tried again. "Kiddo, we can fix it, I promise. It'll be even prettier than before. You'll see."

Still nothing.

Trish took a step back and stared at the closed door, at a loss. She wondered now if this was anything like what her parents must have felt on days when she came home complaining about Ian's treatment of her. She suspected Kelsey's unhappiness ran much deeper than her own ever had, though. And try as she might, she couldn't think of any magical words of wisdom to make everything all better.

She could paint, though, and fix the damage that was done. A drop in the bucket maybe, but one she could add nevertheless. Turning, she left the way she had come.

Outside, Ian had already collected a bucket of water and some rags. He wrung out the first rag just as Trish reappeared on the porch. "Are there any parts we can save?" he asked flatly with a nod toward the ruined winter scene.

"Better to just wipe the slate clean on this one. I've got some stuff in the car that might work better to get that off."

"Were you able to get her to talk?"

Trish shook her head.

Ian slapped the wet rag against the window and began scrubbing with a vehemence that Trish suspected he would have liked to have applied elsewhere.

"Listen," she said briskly. "Can you clean this up on your own while I get started on the other window? Then I can redo this one when I'm finished."

He paused to look at her. "As in—redo it today?"

"Yes."

"That's a lot of painting for one day, isn't it?"

"Guess I'd better get started then." And Trish went to retrieve her supplies from her car. She felt his eyes on her the whole way and realized she didn't mind.

◆ ◆ ◆

FOR THE FIRST HOUR or two, Trish saw no sign of movement behind the curtains in Kelsey's window. She worked with deliberate loudness—clinking paint jars together, wiping parts of the window clean with squeaky scrubbing—but nothing seemed to whet Kelsey's curiosity enough to make the girl peek outside. Undeterred, Trish painted on, glancing frequently at her reference point, namely the image she had printed out from her computer at home and brought with her. She'd managed to smudge paint on its edges, but nothing messy enough to spoil the main picture.

Not bad, she told herself, eyeing her half-finished handiwork. She'd used different paints on this one, colors that would look like stained glass when the sun shone on them, and it was going to be a thing of beauty by the time she was through with it.

She hoped.

Progress was slow, though. It would go faster if she had a small helper at her side. She watched the curtains hopefully and then sighed when they still didn't even so much as flutter.

"That's a griffin."

Trish turned to see Ian standing a few feet behind her. "Oh, good, you can tell what it is. I was afraid it might turn out looking like a weird bird-dog-lion hybrid thing with a bad case of mange."

He came closer, his eyes never leaving the window. "I thought you said you didn't know anything about griffins."

"I do now, thanks to the internet." She held up the paint-smudged printout. "See?"

Ian turned his attention to her. "You researched it?"

"Well..." Trish shrugged. "She did put in a special request, right? Let me tell you, there are a lot of griffins online. They're kind of cool, actually, so it was hard to pick just one, but—" She realized he was staring at her, and she grew self-conscious. "What? Doesn't it look okay?"

"Yes," he said softly. "She'll love it."

"Hope so. Is the front window all cleaned off?"

He nodded, his eyes still on her. Despite the frosty temperature of the air, Trish began to feel warm under his gaze. Funny how warmth like that could send shivers down her spine.

There was a flicker of movement at the edge of one of the curtains then that caught Trish's attention, and a small brown eye looked warily out. It widened, and then both curtains were yanked open as Kelsey caught sight of the half-finished griffin just as a stray sunbeam cut through the clouds to light it up. She stared, openmouthed, and then abruptly turned and disappeared from the window.

Trish blinked. "Is that a good sign or a bad one?" she asked Ian.

"I think it was good," Ian answered with a growing smile, and then he nodded toward the front of the house as the sound of a slamming door cut through the wintery air.

A few seconds later, Kelsey darted around the corner of the house. She hadn't bothered to grab a coat before she came outside, but she didn't seem to notice the cold as she looked intently at the window. "Needs some more feathers," she said finally.

"Yeah, you're probably right. I was thinking it might need a longer tail, too."

Kelsey shook her head, her eyes never leaving the painted figure. "No, you did a good job on the tail."

"Yeah? Thanks. It's not finished yet, but—" Then Trish gasped and nearly lost her balance as Kelsey abruptly threw her arms around Trish's waist. Recovering, Trish hesitated a moment and then let instinct take over as her arms wrapped around the girl's shoulders to return the hug.

"Thanks," Kelsey mumbled against Trish's side, the word muffled by Trish's coat.

"Sure thing, kiddo," Trish returned softly, surprised at the unexpected jolt of emotion she felt. Clearing her throat, she released Kelsey and bent down to look her in the eye. "I could use some help finishing it, though, especially if we're going to get the front window repainted before it gets dark."

Kelsey's eyes dimmed. "But what if it just gets ruined again?"

"Then we'll paint it again."

"But—"

"No one's going to ruin it this time," Ian told his daughter, and there was a hard edge beneath the words that made Trish believe him, although she wondered how he planned to keep that promise.

Kelsey looked back and forth between her father and Trish, and then the rigidity in her small frame finally relaxed. "Okay." She started to reach for a paintbrush with a gleam in her eye.

"Jacket first," her father said, nodding toward the house.

"But—"

"And a hat."

Grumbling under her breath but with her eyes still shining, Kelsey hurried toward the house to comply.

"Impressive grip," Trish observed, putting her hand on her waist where Kelsey had hugged her. "What are you feeding that kid, anyway?"

Ian didn't answer her but only watched her with a sort of wonder in his expression. Or maybe it was something else? She couldn't tell. But it was doing funny things to her insides.

"Well," she said, with an awkward nod toward the window. "Guess I'd better get to work on those missing feathers."

"Not yet."

She did a double take. "I beg your pardon?"

"You haven't taken a break since you got here. Come inside and have some coffee first to warm you up."

"But—"

"Coffee," he repeated in a tone that brooked no argument, and he gently took the paintbrush from her hand and set it down.

And a bemused Trish let him wrap his fingers around hers and lead her inside.

❖ Chapter Six ❖

"THERE," TRISH SAID HOURS later, making the last stroke with her paintbrush and straightening before the front window—or at least straightening as much as she could when her back ached this badly.

Beside her in the evening's darkness, Ian shifted the heavy-duty flashlight he'd been holding for some time now to better illuminate what she was doing. "All done?"

"Man, I hope so, because I think my arm's about ready to fall off."

Together they examined the winter fairyland scene Trish had recreated. Well, Kelsey had recreated some of it, too, but she had long since been sent inside to thaw out by the fireplace, and Trish suspected the little girl was sitting there still and happily devouring a second or even a third cupcake. She had squealed with pleasure at the sight of the fake spiders and vampire teeth, so Trish knew she'd done well with those.

"Looks wonderful," Ian said.

"Let's just hope it stays that way."

"It will."

Trish set down her paintbrush and took off her fingerless gloves—the only kind she could really wear while painting—to blow on her hands and rub them together for warmth. "You planning on camping out on your front porch with a baseball bat?"

"More like sitting up in the living room with a big pot of strong coffee. But the bat's tempting." Ian put the flashlight on the front steps, tugged off his gloves, and then reached to take Trish's hands between his own and warm them. It was a very casual movement that he didn't seem to think twice about, but Trish stood absolutely stock-still like a deer in the headlights. "It's ironic," he added, apparently not noticing her budding catatonia.

Trish reminded herself to breathe, and finally her lungs obeyed her. "Oh?" she managed, feeling the new warmth in her hands begin to spread to other places in her body the longer he massaged her fingers like that.

"Yeah. I was a troubled punk myself as a kid. You'd think that would make me more forgiving."

"But…?"

"But she's my little girl." He released her hands and took a step back. "Better?"

She nodded, all the while sorry he had stopped. "So," she added, with an attempt at lightness and a step back of her own. "You'll be lurking as the Caffeinated Avenger, then? Nice. I'll probably be needing an IV of caffeine myself tomorrow."

"Can't sleep in late?"

"I've got the early shift tomorrow. Got to get up at three."

His eyes widened with what appeared to be genuine horror. "In the *morning*?"

Trish shrugged. "Bakery, remember?" Turning, she started putting lids back on paint jars.

Ian bent to help collect her supplies that were scattered here and there. "You shouldn't have stayed this long. You'll be exhausted tomorrow."

"I wanted to get it done."

He paused. "For Kelsey, you mean."

"Well… yeah."

"Trish?"

"Yes?"

"Thank you. Very much."

She nodded again, wondering if it was exhaustion or his proximity that made it so hard for her to talk suddenly.

"Here," he said, reaching for her brushes. "I'll go rinse these for you."

He disappeared inside the house while Trish packed her supplies in the back seat of her car, but by the time she was done, he was already walking back to her, clean brushes in hand.

"She's out like a light in there," he said wryly. "Right on the couch, and with frosting on her mouth."

"Busy day."

"I'll bring her by your bakery to say thank you, if that's okay."

"Absolutely."

Ian reached into his back pocket to pull something out and hand to her along with her brushes. "For you," he said, and she saw that it was a check.

Trish glanced at the check as she took it and did a double take. "I think this is more than we agreed on."

"I think you *did* more than we agreed on. A lot more."

"You don't have to—"

"Yes, I do." They stood there in silence for a long moment, and then Ian cleared his throat. "Thanks for making her smile."

"My pleasure," Trish told him, meaning it.

"And for the cupcakes." He grinned. "*And* the spiders."

She couldn't help but return his smile. "Went with my instincts on that one."

"Good instincts."

"I try."

"Have dinner with me."

"I—Huh?"

"Have dinner with me," he repeated softly, his eyes holding hers captive.

Trish felt a sudden need for support and leaned back against her car before her knees could give out on her. "Uh…"

"Too blunt? Sorry," he continued ruefully. "I'm a little rusty at this, so…" He trailed off and ran his hands through his hair, looking by all appearances like he was having a very hard time finding the right words for whatever it was he was trying to say.

Actually, Trish thought he was doing quite well, no matter how rusty he thought he might be. "You're asking me out?"

"I'm trying to." Ian's mouth curved upward. "Apparently pretty badly, though."

Her pulse sped up, and her grip on her paintbrushes tightened. "No, you're doing fine."

"Is that a yes?"

Was it? Apparently so, because her head nodded in response before she could quite wrap her mind around the idea of going out on a date with Ian Rafferty. Her body appeared to be running the show now, which was just as well since her mind seemed to have blown a fuse.

"Tomorrow?"

"Okay." At least her mouth was working again.

Ian seemed to notice her mouth, too, because his gaze suddenly dropped to it, and Trish felt a whole new level of heat rush through her.

What surprised her most wasn't the possibility that he might want to kiss her. It was the realization that she wouldn't mind so much if he did.

Startled by her own feelings, she inadvertently loosened her hold on the brushes, and they clattered to the ground. "Oh—"

They both bent to pick them up at the same time and nearly bumped heads. Time to make an exit, Trish decided, taking the paintbrush he held out to her and quickly turning to open her car door.

"Seven o'clock?" he asked her as she got in the driver's side.

"Seven? Yeah, sure." She suddenly pictured him reading her real name by the buzzer at her apartment building, and then she winced inwardly. She was going to have to figure out how to handle the problem of her name soon, but for now... "Why don't you pick me up at the bakery?"

"It's a date."

A date...

Trish pulled away from the curb with more haste than she originally intended and realized her fingers had a death grip on the steering wheel. She loosened them and stared at the road ahead, struggling to see her way in the dark and the swirl of snowflakes.

She had the distinct feeling she was in trouble, and it had nothing to do with the road conditions.

◆ ◆ ◆

SOMEONE NUDGED HER. "HONEY?"

Waking up just enough to turn her face away from whoever was bothering her, Trish mumbled and let her head settle back down on her folded arms.

"Trish!"

"Huh?" Trish forced her bleary eyes open and lifted her head. "What?"

Nadia stood over her, hands on her hips and her eyebrows raised. "You've been asleep at that table for almost an hour. I'd have let you sleep longer, but you were snoring, and it was starting to scare customers."

Blinking, Trish looked around and realized she'd fallen asleep in the middle of wiping down one of the bakery tables. "Shoot, I'm sor—hey, I don't snore."

"Oh, yes you do. And there's another witness to prove it." Nadia gestured behind her, and Trish saw little Mrs. Beasley standing at the counter.

Mrs. Beasley beamed at her and waved a wrinkled hand. "You do, dear. Like a buzz saw."

Muttering under her breath, Trish got up and resumed cleaning the table.

"What happened yesterday?" Nadia asked her, frowning.

"We painted."

"I've never seen you this worn out from painting before. Just how big was his window anyway?"

"Well, we were up kind of late finishing it." Remembering the way the evening ended, Trish felt her cheeks grow warm.

"Oh, my," said Mrs. Beasley, peering at her intently through her impressive glasses. "I think she's blushing."

Nadia's eyes widened. "She *is* blushing. Holy cannoli, girlfriend. What exactly happened last night? And don't you dare leave anything out."

"Nothing happened. But..." The heat in her face grew. "He asked if he could take me to dinner."

Nadia and Mrs. Beasley exchanged a look of pure delight, and for a moment Trish thought they might also do a high-five. Then Nadia looked suddenly worried. "Wait—you said yes, right? Please tell me you said yes."

"I said yes."

"That's fantastic! So why do you look like you're about to face a firing squad?"

"Because I'm tired, and I'm mixed up, and he still doesn't know who I really am." Trish slumped back against the counter and folded her arms across her chest.

"But you do like him."

"Yeah," Trish admitted grudgingly. "I like him."

"Then tell him the truth the next time you see him, because the longer you wait, the weirder it's going to be."

"How about I just get my name legally changed to Acker? It'd be simpler."

Her friend frowned and studied her. "What's scary is that I'm not entirely sure you're joking." She put her arm around Trish's shoulders and gave her an encouraging squeeze. "It'll be okay, Trish. Just stay calm, take a few deep breaths, and tell him the whole story."

"I don't have a good track record of staying calm around him."

"Well, you could always zip over to Vegas with him for the weekend, and get your name legally changed to Rafferty. Problem solved."

"You're a fruitcake."

"No, I'm a romantic. So when is this big dinner date happening?"

Trish tried one of those deep, calming breaths. "Tonight."

"Tonight?" Nadia gasped and clapped her hands to her cheeks, clearly appalled. "But you look awful! Look at you, bags under your eyes, all bloodshot—"

"Gee, thanks. Now I'm not nervous at all."

Her friend abruptly whipped Trish's apron off of her and grabbed her coat and purse. "Go home and get some sleep. And maybe give yourself a quick facial, too."

"Tea bags," Mrs. Beasley suggested anxiously. "She needs tea bags for her eyes."

Pausing long enough to grab a handful of unopened tea bags from behind the counter and thrust them into Trish's hands, Nadia firmly escorted Trish to the door.

"But—"

"Go," Nadia insisted. "Sleep."

"I'm too nervous to sleep now," Trish returned, her pulse speeding up just at the thought of dinner tonight.

"Try anyway." Nadia held the front door open for her. "And Trish? Try to let yourself have a little fun tonight." Then she grinned. "But don't do anything I wouldn't do, girlfriend."

"That doesn't narrow it down much," Trish called back over her shoulder as she started down the sidewalk.

CHRISTINE S. FELDMAN

❖ Chapter Seven ❖

AS IT TURNED OUT, she could sleep, and if she hadn't set her alarm for five o'clock, she probably would have kept right on sleeping. But now, two hours later, she was standing alone inside the locked bakery and pacing in front of the windows as she waited for Ian and tried to figure out the best way to explain their previous history to him.

Funny story... you used to pick on me when we were kids and I hated your guts, so I planned to re-enter your life under false pretenses and get some revenge, but now I think I really like you, and I'd like to pretend none of that ever happened. So... want to split an appetizer?

A knock on the window startled her from her train of thought, and she looked up to see Ian standing outside on the sidewalk. He smiled at her through the glass, and she flashed a nervous smile in return, thinking that for a man who claimed he'd been out of the dating game for a while, he certainly cleaned up nicely. His shirt was open at the collar, but he wore an honest to goodness suit jacket over it, and she tried unsuccessfully to recall the last time she'd gone out with a man who actually made an effort to look good on her account.

"Hi," he greeted her as she stepped outside.

"Hey," she returned, her pulse already fluttering. *Knock it off, Trish. Keep your head on straight.*

His eyes flitted over her. "You look… very nice."

And that's why women still wore skirts in winter, Trish thought. No matter how cold it might get. "Thanks," she said, smoothing out nonexistent wrinkles in the sweater dress that showed off her legs to great advantage.

"Although I'll admit I do like the way you look in paint splatters."

"I'll bet you say that to all the girls."

He grinned, and Trish let herself smile back, praying it didn't come across quite as goofy or adolescent as she feared. Their eyes held each other's for a moment before Ian broke the silence again. "Ready?"

Man, I hope so, she thought but outwardly only nodded, and he opened the passenger's side door of his car for her.

"Do you like Italian food?" he asked after he got in and started the engine.

"Love it."

"Good, because there's this little Italian place I heard about..."

And a few minutes later they pulled up to the curb near La Bella Rosa. Trish felt her mouth turn up slightly at the corners.

"Have you eaten here before?" Ian asked her, catching her faint smile.

"It's like a second home," she admitted. "You've really never been here?"

"Kelsey's usually the one who picks the restaurants for us. If it doesn't have a kiddy meal with a toy inside, we don't go. Sorry—You want to go somewhere else?"

Surprised, Trish glanced at Ian and caught a flicker of chagrin in his expression. "No, not at all," she said quickly, and it suddenly occurred to her that she might not be the only one who was nervous tonight. Her heart did a pleasant sort of skip. "I already know I love the food here. What's not to like about that?"

"You sure?"

"Positive," she assured him, and to prove her point, she opened the passenger door and stepped out.

Getting out to join her, Ian offered her his arm. "Sidewalk's slippery."

Trish hesitantly slid her arm through his and realized that the sidewalk wasn't her problem. It was more the way that their close proximity made her suddenly aware of the warmth radiating from his body and of the faint trace of cologne that he wore. Or was it aftershave? Whatever it was, it made her dangerously lightheaded, forcing her to hold on to him tightly.

Well, there were worse things that could happen to a girl, she thought as they walked toward La Bella Rosa.

A waitress sat them at a table up front and center, not far from a window. Snow on the ground glowed in dim light cast by twinkling Christmas lights strung up outside, and a few tiny snowflakes were just starting to fall from the night sky. All in all, not a bad setting for a romantic dinner for two. Which made Trish wonder, actually, about where a certain third party might be. "Where's Kelsey tonight?" Trish asked, sliding off her coat.

"With a neighbor. I think she plans to spend the entire evening glued to the woman's front window so she can keep an eye on ours. Well, at least until *my* shift starts."

"Any trouble with vandals last night?"

He shook his head with obvious relief, and for the first time Trish noticed the shadows under his eyes.

"You really did stay up last night to guard it, didn't you?" she asked.

"Tried to. Nodded off a couple of times, in spite of all the caffeine. I haven't pulled an all-nighter since college." He grinned. "Guess I'm a little rusty at that, too."

"We probably should have waited for a later night to do this."

"And give you time to change your mind? Couldn't risk it."

Trish returned his smile from across the table. Neither of them looked away, and a delicious sort of shiver travelled through Trish that only grew more intense when her leg accidentally brushed against Ian's under the tabletop. It had been a long time since she'd experienced a shiver like that, the kind of shiver that made a girl believe that her evening could possibly end very well.

"I'm glad you said yes to tonight," Ian told her, his eyes still on hers.

There was that shiver again. And that look he was giving her...that was a look a woman could get used to. "Me, too."

He cleared his throat. "Trish..."

But a familiar voice interrupted him before he could finish whatever he was about to say, much to Trish's disappointment. "Ah, there's my girl. *Buonasera.* Where have you been?"

Trish looked up to see Pop De Luca beaming at her. Her disappointment softened. "Hi, Pop."

Pop pressed a hand to his heart as if wounded. "'Hi, Pop' she says to me," he complained to Ian. "It's been a week since I've laid eyes on her, and all she says is 'Hi, Pop.'" He frowned at Trish. "The last time you went that long without coming to La Bella, you were laid up with the flu. You been sick, *cara*? I would have sent you soup, you know. Nothing better than a bowl of my *zuppa Toscana* to get you back on your feet."

Ian gave Trish a startled glance. "'Pop'? Your family owns this restaurant?"

"No, Pop is everybody's Pop. And no, I haven't been sick," she assured the old man, getting up to give him an affectionate hug. "Just busy."

"Too busy to eat?"

"I think a lot of that has been my fault," Ian said, rising from his seat and extending his hand. "I've been taking up a lot of her time lately. Hi. Ian Rafferty."

The old man started to shake hands. "Ian Rafferty? Now where have I heard—" He stopped and frowned.

Trish suddenly flashed back to the other day when she and Nadia had eaten here, and Pop's voice echoed in her head. *Give me his name, I'll talk to the pazzo and set him straight...*

Her eyes widened. "Wait, Pop—"

But Pop was already speaking. "*You're* the bum?" he said to Ian, giving him a disgruntled once-over.

Ian blinked. "I'm the what?"

No, no, no... "Pop," Trish repeated urgently, putting her hand on his arm and trying unsuccessfully to turn his attention to her instead. "You don't understand. It's not like that."

"Not like what?" Ian asked, his confusion clearly growing by the second.

The old man wrinkled his brow. "He's not a bum?"

"No, he's not," Trish insisted, feeling her face grow warm.

"He apologize to you yet?"

"No, but—"

"Then he's a bum!"

"Apologize for what?" Ian asked, glancing back and forth between both of them. "What's going on?"

"Nothing," said Trish hastily, wishing the ground would open up and swallow her. Torn between her desire to spare the old man's feelings and her need to make him leave before she spontaneously combusted from mortification, she tried again. "Pop, I know you mean well, and please don't take this the wrong way, but please—*please*—trust me on this and let it go?"

"But—"

"*Pop*!"

Pop looked dissatisfied, but after another pleading look from Trish, he finally threw his hands up in the air in defeat. "Have it your way, *cara*," he grumbled. "But while he's in my restaurant, he'd better treat you right, or I'm tossing him out the door myself." And he grudgingly headed back toward the kitchen, but not before giving Ian an I'm-keeping-my-eye-on-you gesture.

Ian stared after Pop's departing figure before finally turning wide eyes onto Trish. "What was that all about?"

She swallowed, her mouth growing dry. "Pop is a little... protective."

"A little? I think he wants to put my spleen on the menu. Has he just got me confused with somebody else?"

For a moment Trish was sorely tempted to simply say yes and try to recapture the earlier mood, but she was sane enough to admit to herself that wasn't terribly realistic. No, thanks to a well-meaning Pop, the door to her history with Ian had been flung wide open, and there was little else to do now but go through it. Unless she faked a heart attack, which—for a moment—she considered doing.

"Not exactly," she said finally, sinking back into her seat with all the joy of a student who'd been sent to the principal's office for bad behavior.

Ian did a double take. "What?"

"Look, this is going to sound a little strange—"

"Stranger than what just happened?"

Trish winced inwardly. "There's something I was planning to tell you tonight, just not quite like this." *Understatement of the year.* "Or at least not with Pop's help."

Now Ian looked wary as well as bewildered. Great. If she wasn't coming off like a kook yet, she probably would soon.

She took a deep breath. "You and I... we've actually met before."

"We have?"

"Yes."

Ian frowned and studied her. "I think I would remember you, Trish."

Sweet, she thought wistfully. "Yeah, that's another thing. Trish is short for Patricia." Her stomach started to churn. Wonderful. Perhaps she could put the icing on the cake and wind up throwing up on his shoes out of nervousness. Perfect way to cap off the evening. She forced herself to look him in the eye. "And my last name's not Acker. It's Ackerly. You just sort of misheard it the first time, and I never corrected you."

He stared at her blankly.

"You might remember me better as Pattycake." Heat blossomed in her cheeks again as she felt a wave of fresh embarrassment. "But I look a little different now than I used to back when we were in grade school together."

"Grade school? But—" His eyes widened abruptly with dawning comprehension. "Patricia... *Ackerly?*"

Biting her lip, she nodded.

"No..." he breathed, his expression flickering first to shock and then dismay.

And there went her stomach again, Trish thought. "I'm sorry," she said, standing up a little too quickly and feeling lightheaded as a result. She clutched the table to regain her balance, all the while feeling the eyes of curious diners turn toward her. "I shouldn't have... You know, I think I need a little air."

"Trish—"

"No, really, I do," she insisted, grabbing her coat and purse and then backing away from the table and Ian. "Because those look like really nice shoes, and I'd hate to ruin them."

"Hate to—what?"

But she was already hurrying toward the restaurant's exit and away from her growing audience.

The blast of cold air that hit her as soon as she stepped outside did wonders both to clear her head and cool her flaming cheeks. She inhaled deeply and closed her eyes, willing her stomach to return to normal before she faced Ian again and suspecting she didn't have a whole lot of time before that happened.

And she was right, because a moment later she heard the buzz of restaurant noise as the door opened again briefly, and she knew he was right behind her.

"Trish—Patricia—"

"Trish," she said over her shoulder. "I haven't liked the name Patricia since I was a kid."

"Because... of me." It was a statement more than it was a question.

Trish shrugged, and silence stretched out between them for what felt like an eternity before Ian spoke again.

"When did you realize who I was?" he asked finally.

"From the start."

"Why didn't you say anything?"

"I planned to," she admitted. She still refused to look at him, but she could feel his eyes on her. "That first day. And I planned to tell you off but *good*."

"So why didn't you?"

She shivered and realized she was still clutching her coat in her arms instead of wearing it. Somehow she couldn't bring herself to budge, though. "Because of Kelsey. And because... because things changed."

Ian saw the shiver. He reached for the coat in her arms to drape it over her shoulders, and even with the awkwardness of their situation, the gesture struck Trish as sweetly solicitous. "You got your teeth fixed."

"Yeah."

"I liked that crooked little tooth," he said softly.

An incredulous and mirthless little laugh escaped her, and she stared at him. "Liked it? What are you talking about? You used to make fun of it all the time."

It was his turn to look away. "I remember."

"You teased me about everything back then. My hair, my teeth, my name—Why did you do that?"

"Because when you're twelve years old, you can be kind of stupid when it comes to showing a girl you like her."

"That's no excu—what?" She blinked, sure she hadn't heard him right.

"I had a huge crush on you. You honestly had no idea?"

Flabbergasted, she shook her head. "No, I admit that you tripping me and pulling my hair didn't clue me in."

The light from the restaurant's entryway was bright enough for Ian's blush to be visible, even at this hour of the evening. "I'm sorry. I was kind of a little rat bastard back then, and I know it."

"Yeah, you were," she agreed.

Ian was silent for a moment, and then she felt rather than saw a new kind of tension fill him. Finally he pointed to the faint scar above his eye, and cleared his throat. "Did you ever hear the story about how I got this?"

The change in subjects startled her. "I think some kids said you were in a gang fight or something."

He chuckled faintly, but there was no humor in the sound. "A gang fight? No. My father gave it to me."

"Your dad?" Trish drew a blank. Neither Ian's father or his mother had ever come to any school functions that she could remember, and she knew nothing about either one of them. For all she'd known, he could have been raised by wolves.

"He was aiming the bottle at my mother but got me instead. They were having a fight about something, probably over whose turn it was to light up next."

She stared at him, speechless.

"There was a lot of fighting and yelling. And worse." He ran a hand through his hair and shrugged ruefully. "But that's pretty much all I had to go off of back then, so my social skills were—well... lacking. Doesn't excuse my behavior, but maybe it helps explain it. I'm sorry, Trish. I was a miserable kid, and I made people around me miserable then, too."

In light of his revelation, the past took on a slightly different cast. The sullen attitude, the standoffishness... "Oh," Trish said softly.

"Somebody called the cops after one of my parents' fights one night. Long story short, I ended up going into foster care. My foster parents are the reason I got my head on straight."

"Foster care?" Something clicked in her mind. "That's why you moved away so suddenly."

"Yes."

Snowflakes began to fall thick and fast, sticking to the pavement in front of their feet and making lovely, swirling patterns.

"You used to paint then, too," Ian said abruptly. "I remember a mural on a wall at school. You painted an ocean scene, didn't you? With whales?"

He remembered that? She barely remembered that herself. "Dolphins," Trish said after a minute, searching her memory. "I was big into dolphins then.

And unicorns. Made for quite an interesting mural, I'll say that much."

"It was beautiful, and I didn't have a lot of beauty in my life back then. I remember thinking you'd have to be somebody pretty special to paint something like that," Ian said, looking at her. "And I was right."

It was back, Trish thought with a little flutter of pleasure as they held each other's gazes. That look from the restaurant, the one he'd given her before everything went south. Could it be he didn't think she was totally wacko after all? "Special, good? Or special as in 'back away from her slowly'?"

"Special as in the kind of woman who drops everything to give a little girl a special Christmas treat even if she thinks the girl's dad is—I'm sorry, what was it again? A bum?"

A startled laugh escaped her before she could stop it, and she was sure she blushed again. "Sorry about what happened in there with Pop," Trish told him after a minute, nodding back toward the restaurant. "And for not explaining things sooner. I just wasn't sure how to do it."

"I'm sorry I used to be a such a little—well, you know." Ian cleared his throat. "Maybe… we could start over?"

"Start over?"

"Yes." He held out his hand to her. "Give me a chance to make things up to you?"

Relief poured through her. "I'd like that." And she put her hand in his as if to shake it.

His fingers closed around hers, and for such an innocent kind of contact, it left Trish's pulse racing much faster than before. Neither of them pulled their hand back, and they remained there with their eyes locked on each other's until finally Trish felt Ian pull her ever so gently toward him. She went willingly, her breath catching in her throat as she saw his gaze drop to her mouth.

But the door to the restaurant opened then to let a laughing foursome out, and a startled Trish was forced to let go of Ian's hand and step back to avoid being caught in their path. There were two couples, jovial, noisy, and apparently oblivious to the moment they had just interrupted. They paused, inadvertently becoming a barrier between her and the man she was fairly certain had been two seconds away from kissing her. And it would have been a good kiss, too, she could tell. Very good.

She sighed inwardly.

One of the men erupted in guffaws over something the other said, and rather than going anywhere, he clapped his arm around the other man's shoulders as if he intended to stay in huddle formation.

Trish reminded herself that it was Christmastime, and that she ought to be charitable and full of good cheer, but as the group remained exactly where they were and seemed to be in no apparent hurry to leave, she felt her holiday spirit rapidly disintegrating. Surely they would move along to their cars now, surely they would want to get out of the cold and take their party somewhere warm and bright? Surely they could feel waves of frustration emanating from her direction as she waited to be alone with Ian again—

"Excuse me," she heard Ian say over the noise. "Could I get you folks to move just a few feet over that way? There's a beautiful woman on the other side of you, and I've waited almost twenty years to kiss her."

Trish blinked as all conversation stopped and four pairs of eyes swiveled to look in her direction. Yes, tonight was certainly her night for blushing. She lifted one hand in a self-conscious little wave.

"Oh, is there mistletoe?" one of the women asked, searching above her to see if some hung from the covered walkway. "I love mistletoe!"

The man beside her started chuckling and motioned for his group to move along, which they did with knowing smiles on their faces.

And then Ian walked slowly over to where Trish stood. She glanced overhead. "There's no mistletoe here."

"Mistletoe is for amateurs," he informed her with a look in his eye that made her knees go just a little bit weak, and he put his arms around her waist to bring her closer as he bent his head to kiss her.

And Trish discovered that for someone whose mouth used to say such sour things to her as a child, Ian Rafferty certainly knew how to do some very sweet things with his lips now.

❖ Epilogue ❖

"NOW *THAT* IS A Christmas tree," Trish declared, arranging one last handful of tinsel and stepping back to admire the five-footer they had put up in Ian's living room to replace the sad little shrub he'd had there before. "See how much better that is?"

"Absolutely," Ian agreed, coming up behind her and sliding his arms around her waist. "I'm ashamed I ever had the other one in my home."

"Ah, then my work here is done."

"Does that mean you can play now?" he murmured against her neck, and she started to turn her face toward his to kiss him when Kelsey—who had been preoccupied with adjusting tinsel on the window side of the tree—popped out from behind the evergreen.

Ian and Trish both cleared their throats and abruptly switched to holding hands before the little girl could spot them nuzzling each other.

"It looks awesome!" Kelsey exclaimed. "But couldn't we—"

"No zombie tree topper, Kels."

She grumbled halfheartedly but couldn't seem to muster up much in the way of displeasure at his answer judging by the way her mouth curved upward every time she glanced at the newly decorated Christmas tree. Plopping down into a nearby easy chair, Kelsey alternated her gaze between the tree and the window scene, which showed up nicely in the light from the nearly full moon outside and had remained untouched by vandals. The girl sighed with obvious pleasure.

"She's wearing you down, isn't she?" Trish asked, her voice low so only Ian could hear her. "There are going to be little zombie cupids all over the place here come Valentine's Day."

"Guess you'll have to stick around and find out," he murmured back, giving her a sideways glance that was full of shiver-inducing promise.

Oh, yes, Trish thought, curling her fingers around his. A girl could really get used to this…

The End

PASTELS AND JINGLE BELLS

Author's Note

Thank you for reading <u>Pastels and Jingle Bells</u>! I hope you enjoyed the story. Now that you've read it, I hope you'll consider leaving a review because reviews are a great way for readers to discover new books. I would sincerely appreciate it!

About the Author

Christine S. Feldman writes both novels and feature-length screenplays, and she has placed in screenwriting competitions on both coasts. She lives in the Pacific Northwest with her ballroom-dancing husband and their beagle. Visit her on Facebook at https://www.facebook.com/ChristineSFeldman or follow her on Twitter at https://twitter.com/FeldmanCS.

Discover other titles from Christine S. Feldman:

Coming Home

The Bargain

Heavenly Bites Novella #1: Pastels and Jingle Bells

Heavenly Bites Novella #2: Love Lessons

Heavenly Bites Novella #3: Playing Cupid

All's Fair in Love and Weddings

Winging It

The Encore

It Happened One Night (Adventures in Blind Dating #1)

Center Stage (Adventures in Blind Dating #2)

The Fix-Up Mix-Up (Adventures in Blind Dating #3)